The Few

Samuel D. Hunter

A Samuel French Acting Edition

SAMUELFRENCH.COM
SAMUELFRENCH-LONDON.CO.UK

FOR PRODUCTION ENQUIRIES

UNITED STATES AND CANADA

Info@SamuelFrench.com
1-866-598-8449

UNITED KINGDOM AND EUROPE

Plays@SamuelFrench-London.co.uk
020-7255-4302

Each title is subject to availability from Samuel French, depending upon
country of performance. Please be aware that *THE FEW* may not be
licensed by Samuel French in your territory. Professional and amateur
producers should contact the nearest Samuel French office or licensing
partner to verify availability.

MUSIC USE NOTE

THE FEW received its world premiere at The Old Globe in San Diego, CA in October, 2013. The production was directed by Davis McCallum, with sets by Dane Laffrey, costumes by Jessica Pabst, lights by Matt Frey, and original music and sound by Daniel Kluger. The Production Stage Manager was Annette Yé. The cast was as follows:

BRYAN	Michael Laurence
QZ	Eva Kaminsky
MATTHEW	Gideon Glick
FEMALE VOICE 2	Jenny Bacon

THE FEW received its New York premiere at Rattlestick Playwrights Theater in April, 2014. The production was directed by Davis McCallum, with sets by Dane Laffrey, costumes by Jessica Pabst, lights by Eric Southern, original music and sound by Daniel Kluger, and props by Andrew Diaz. The Production Manager was Eugenia Furneaux, the Production Stage Manager was Katharine Whitney, and the Assistant Stage Manager was Emily Cates. The cast was as follows:

BRYAN	Michael Laurence
QZ	Tasha Lawrence
MATTHEW	Gideon Glick
FEMALE VOICE 2	Jenny Bacon

Additional development and workshops were done at:

The Playwrights Center, directed by Kip Fagan (February 2012)

2012 Pacific Playwrights Festival at South Coast Repertory, directed by Casey Stangl (April 2012)

2012 Perry-Mansfield New Works Festival, directed by Casey Stangl (June 2012)

Williamstown Theater Festival, directed by Adam Rapp (July 2012)

JAW West at Portland Center Stage, directed by Stella Powell-Jones (July 2012)

CHARACTERS

BRYAN – Late thirties to mid-forties, male
QZ – Late thirties to mid-forties, female
MATTHEW – Nineteen, male

TEN MALE VOICES
SIX FEMALE VOICES

TIME

August, 1999.

SETTING

The inside of a weathered, paper-littered, unkempt office space off of some random exit on I-90 in northern Idaho. The whole room should feel like a manufactured home – maybe even a converted double-wide. There are a few desks with aging desktop computers on top, piles of newspapers, a sad, dying fern here and there. There is an unseen back room and bathroom offstage.

AUTHOR'S NOTES

Dialogue written in italics is emphatic, deliberate; dialogue in ALL CAPS is impulsive, explosive.

A "/" indicates an overlap in dialogue. Whenever a "/" appears, the following line of dialogue should begin.

Ellipses (…) indicate when a character is trailing off, dashes (–) indicate where a character is being cut off, either by another character or themselves.

No intermission.

Dedicated to the memory of Seamus O'Bryan

Scene One

(Mid-day.)

(QZ sits at one of the desks, BRYAN sits across from her, mud splattered over his shirt.)

(QZ stares at him coldly. In the silence, BRYAN pulls out a pack of cigarettes.)

QZ. Don't smoke in here.

BRYAN. Since when?

(QZ stares at him. BRYAN puts the cigarettes away. A silence between them.)

(QZ grabs a newspaper off of her desk, reads.)

QZ. *(reading)* "The fact is, when our computers hit midnight in four short months and suddenly their internal clocks think the year is 1900, we don't know what will happen. Will planes fall out of the sky? Will there be world-wide blackouts? At the very least, we can definitely say that the Y2K bug could quite certainly plunge us into a worldwide depression. But whatever happens, I can only hope that we start to re-examine how much of our daily lives rely on these fallible machines."

(QZ puts the paper down.)

BRYAN. Wow, QZ.

QZ. I know. I know it.

BRYAN. That was / really –

QZ. You see how it sounds like an *actual newspaper* now? You see how it / actually – ?

BRYAN. Sure.

(pause)

QZ. I've been seeing someone else.

BRYAN. Okay.

QZ. I ran my own personal ad in the paper a while ago, we started writing one another. It's amazing, he's actually better than you in every way imaginable. I mean, there is not a single way in which he is not better than you.

BRYAN. That's – good.

QZ. His letters to me are *amazing*. Poetry. For *me*.

(Silence. She stares at him.)

(re: his dirty shirt)

How'd that happen?

BRYAN. Oh, it's just –. Happened last night –

(The phone rings.)

I was trying to get a ride on the side of the highway, truck hit a puddle and / I got –

QZ. You *hitchhiked* here? What happened to the Toyota?

(The phone rings again.)

BRYAN. Oh that thing hasn't –. Stopped running about a year after I – …

(The phone rings one last time.)

(The answering machine picks up. **QZ** *exits to the back.)*

VOICE OF QZ. Hello love seekers! You've reached the message line for *The Few*'s personal ad section. Please leave your name, phone number, location, and your personal ad exactly as you would like it printed. Someone will call you back soon for payment information. Happy hunting!

*(***QZ*** *re-enters. She tosses* **BRYAN** *a clean flannel shirt.* **BRYAN** *catches it, changes his shirt.)*

(The answering machine beeps.)

MALE VOICE 1. Hey there. Danny callin' again, QZ has my payment info, Eastern Oregon, 541-235-2950. Looking for lady co-pilot to navigate end times. Spacious bunker with comfortable bed, running water, tape deck. Can withstand four-megaton blast. Me: over sixty. You: under forty. Let's ride!

(pause)

QZ. You're thin.

BRYAN. I am?

QZ. Yeah, you –. Yeah.

BRYAN. I guess I – haven't been taking very good care of myself.

(pause)

QZ. Milo died.

BRYAN. Oh, okay. How'd he die?

QZ. Ran out onto the interstate.

BRYAN. Oh, that's –. Did you bury him?

QZ. *Bury* him? How would I get to him? He was in the middle of the interstate. It was awful, too, these trucks just kept driving over him again and again, pretty much spread him evenly from here to mile 436. Didn't rain forever that summer, thank God when it finally did. Washed the stains of him off the road.

(pause)

BRYAN. I remember when we got Milo. That little girl was giving away kittens at the rest stop, and you went up to her / and –

QZ. You don't have anywhere else to go?

(pause)

BRYAN. No, I just –. Really needed to come back.

(Tense silence. They stare at one another.)

BRYAN. *(cont.)* I mean it's –. I mean, it's still my paper.

QZ. Excuse me?

BRYAN. I don't mean –. I'm just saying *legally,* it's still – mine, I still own it. I still own / this trailer –

QZ. This is not the same paper the three of us started here. This is something entirely different. It had to be different, your idea sucked.

BRYAN. C'mon, you believed in it just as much / we did –

QZ. Well, truckers don't want the long-winded, unreadable crap we were giving them. What they want is to post and respond to personal ads.

BRYAN. You used to tell me that we were saving these guys lives, you / always –

QZ. Why are you here, Bryan?

(pause)

BRYAN. You said yourself, maybe we don't have much time left. God knows what's gonna happen, the millennium and everything. Maybe I just – wanted to come back before the world blows up.

QZ. You think you're funny?

BRYAN. I'm not trying / to be –

QZ. You can take your stuff, it's all boxed up in the back. If you need a place to stay, there's a new Econo Lodge off exit 425. Ask for Trista, tell her you know me, she'll give you a deal.

BRYAN. I was thinking I would just sleep here.

QZ. What?

BRYAN. I'll just sleep here, QZ, in the office. You still have Jim's old army cot?

QZ. *No,* that is not happening, that is not – …

(pause)

You left four years ago without a *word*, without saying anything to me, and now you just want to waltz back in here and –

(**BRYAN** stands.)

BRYAN. Look QZ, to be honest I'm sort of at the end of my rope here, I sort of –. I know it was awful of me to walk outta here, I know it, but – ...

(pause)

You're the only person I have left?

*(Pause. **QZ** stares at him.)*

*(Finally, **BRYAN** turns to the door, grabbing his things.)*

I'm sorry, I'll just go, I didn't mean / to –

QZ. No, just – ...

(**BRYAN** *stops.* **QZ** *looks at him.*)

Cot's still in the closet. Goddammit.

(pause)

Listen, if you're gonna stay here a few nights then you're going to *work*, okay? We're behind with the layouts, you can finish those and help with the drop-offs. You're not just gonna come back here and sponge off me, *no way*.

BRYAN. That's fine.

QZ. And we're not changing anything about the paper, you're not gonna write for it, you're not gonna start inviting any long-haul guys over here. The paper works now, we're not changing it back to what it used to be.

BRYAN. Okay.

(pause)

QZ. We use new programs now. Distribution is a lot more than four years ago. You'll be doing the longer drop-offs. And you'll be paying for your own gas. We go as far as South Dakota now.

BRYAN. Oh neat.

QZ. Shut up.

> (**QZ** *grabs a newspaper off her desk, throws it to* **BRYAN**.)

Layout's all different, too. Now we lead off with the personal ads. We've got twelve to fifteen pages of personals, only a couple pages of content. Horoscopes and my column, that's it for content. Thirty percent ad coverage in personals, twenty percent in content.

BRYAN. Where do you get the horoscopes?

QZ. I make 'em up.

BRYAN. Okay.

> (*pause*)

QZ. Bryan, it's not – ... It's not the same paper we started here with Jim.

> (*pause*)

BRYAN. (*looking at the front page*) You kept our title.

QZ. It's a shitty title. "The Few"?

BRYAN. But you kept it.

> (*looking at the paper.*)

It looks good.

QZ. Uh huh.

BRYAN. Formatting's okay. Some of the artwork is pixilated.

> (*reading.*)

You still mix your tenses.

> (**QZ** *grabs the paper out of his hand, throwing it back on her desk.*)

QZ. There's a few stacks in the Honda that need to be delivered, do that now. The McDonald's off 489, you remember?

BRYAN. Sure.

(**BRYAN** *heads toward the door. Just before he's out the door,* **QZ** *stands up.*)

QZ. Wait.

(**BRYAN** *stops.*)

Bryan, what are you – ...? How long are we gonna do this?

(*pause*)

Tell me why you're back here.

(*Pause.* **BRYAN** *turns to* **QZ**.)

Tell me why you're back, Bryan. Right now.

(*They stare at one another. An irrationally long silence.*)

BRYAN. QZ, I'm –

(*The phone rings.* **BRYAN** *and* **QZ** *continue to stare at one another.*)

(*The phone rings again. And again.*)

I'm gonna go do the drop-offs.

(**BRYAN** *exits.* **QZ** *watches him leave.*)

(*The phone rings again.*)

Scene Two

*(Later that day. **MATTHEW** sits at one of the desks sorting mail. **BRYAN** enters from outside, stops when he sees **MATTHEW**.)*

MATTHEW. Hi!

(pause)

QZ said – she said she'd like you to finish the layout for the ads on page seven? If that's – ...?

(pause)

I'm – Matthew?

*(Pause. **BRYAN** looks away, slowly making his way inside. He sits at a desk, turns on the computer. He waits for it to start up. **MATTHEW** continues sorting letters.)*

(silence)

I've, uh. I've been working here a few years now? Like since you left, I've been working on the paper since you –.

(pause)

The distribution, you know. It started to pick up, and QZ needed, uh – she wanted help with –.

(pause)

It's cool that you're back though! Yeah.

(pause)

BRYAN. Well I can take it from here, so. You can go.

(pause)

MATTHEW. Wait, what?

BRYAN. Look, things are probably gonna get a little jumpy around here, so why don't you just – go home for a few days.

MATTHEW. Oh see – this is kind of like – my *job*. Like, this is how I make money.

(pause)

Were you and QZ, like, married?

BRYAN. She tell you that?

MATTHEW. No, she –. I just never really figured out what –.

(short pause)

I've, uh –. I've read a lot of the articles you used to
write. A lot of the articles you and Jim used to write,
I used to read them.

BRYAN. What were you, like five years old?

MATTHEW. I'm nineteen, I was like fifteen.

(pause, then quickly)

So – where have you been all this time?! I think I always
figured you were traveling, like exploring the country
or something, or –. Have you been writing the whole
time? I mean if you have *four years* worth of writing
then that's – that's amazing, I bet you've / gotta have –

BRYAN. I'm gonna work on the layout for page seven now.

MATTHEW. Oh. Cool, um.

(BRYAN *goes back to the computer, pulls out a cigarette,
lights it up. He smokes a bit,* **MATTHEW** *looks at him.)*

Could you – ?

BRYAN. I'm working now.

MATTHEW. QZ says people can't smoke in here.

(pause)

BRYAN. What?

MATTHEW. Like, she doesn't want people to smoke? She
says she doesn't want people smoking in here.

(pause)

BRYAN. I own this trailer, I can smoke here if I want.

MATTHEW. The thing is, I'm sort of allergic?

(pause)

BRYAN. No you're not.

MATTHEW. No, I really am.

BRYAN. No one's allergic to cigarette smoke.

MATTHEW. No seriously. Cigarettes and some animals, that's what does it. Went to a rodeo when I was a kid, almost died. Went to the emergency room.

*(**BRYAN** looks at him for a moment, then takes a puff of his cigarette. He continues to smoke as he works on the computer.)*

*(Silence as **MATTHEW** goes back to his work, defeated. Suddenly **MATTHEW** stands up, taking out his wallet. He takes a small newspaper clipping out of his wallet and begins to read, a little nervous.)*

(reading)

"You can find us in between Wallace and Mullan, off exit 419, about two miles south of the gas station. If you ask us what our agenda is, we'll tell you that we don't know. If you ask us why we started a newspaper for truckers, we'll tell you it's because we had to. Because after – "

BRYAN. Stop.

(pause)

Why do you have / that?

MATTHEW. I'm Jim's nephew. *Was* his – ...

(pause)

BRYAN. You're – ...?

MATTHEW. Yeah.

(pause)

I met you, once. At Jim's funeral?

(silence)

*(**BRYAN** puts out his cigarette.)*

MATTHEW. And there's actually a nice little memorial near the bridge where it happened, if you've never seen it – it's like this series of crosses, one for Jim, and then a few for the people in the other car, it's really – …

(pause)

BRYAN. You from Mullan?

MATTHEW. Yeah.

BRYAN. I grew up there.

MATTHEW. Yeah, I know.

BRYAN. You like it?

MATTHEW. It's okay.

BRYAN. I fucking hated it.

MATTHEW. Yeah, well, it's –. I hate it too.

BRYAN. You go to Mullan High?

MATTHEW. Yeah. I fucking hated it.

BRYAN. I thought it was okay.

MATTHEW. Yeah it was okay I guess.

(pause)

BRYAN. I started a poetry club with a friend of mine. Used to publish a little book thingie every semester, they still do that?

MATTHEW. Yeah, actually, I –. I used to edit it.

BRYAN. Really?

MATTHEW. Yeah, it's sort of – my thing. Poetry. I mean I'm not like a *poet*, but I like – write poems?

BRYAN. You drive all the way out here every day from Mullan?

MATTHEW. No, I. I sorta live here.

BRYAN. You – …?

MATTHEW. Yeah, the old airstream next to QZ's trailer, I sort of –. It's okay, sorta hot in the summer, but –.

(pause)

MATTHEW. *(cont.)* Look, I know I –. It must be weird to show up and I'm here, and you don't remember me, but –. When I started reading *The Few*, things were pretty bad for me, my step-dad – ... Anyway, I sorta hated life? But I read your articles, and it was like –. I'd never read anything like that, it –. It was really – important to me. Still is.

(BRYAN *looks at him.)*

BRYAN. Really?

MATTHEW. Yeah, and not just me! Sometimes, when I'm doing drop-offs, I run into some of the truckers who would stop by here during their runs. They see me dropping off copies of the paper, and they come to me and they tell me these stories, how they felt like you and Jim and QZ saved their *lives*, that you –. One guy I met, I think his name was Lance? You remember him?

(pause)

BRYAN. Yeah.

MATTHEW. He told me that when his wife died, and he was doing these seven-thousand mile runs by himself – he felt like you guys were the only family he had. He said he probably wouldn't even be alive anymore if it wasn't for the paper.

BRYAN. It was – something pretty special back then.

MATTHEW. Right! And now that you're here, we can get back to what it used to be! To what it used to do for all these guys. I don't know where you've been, but I bet you've, like – I mean I bet you saw, like, the heart of America, and now – you can write about it. Yeah?

(BRYAN *looks at him.* **QZ** *enters with a stack of mail in her hands and an open envelope.)*

QZ. Matty, I need you to call Bruneel Tires, we can't run this ad – the artwork is terrible, you can't even read the copy –

BRYAN. Send him home, QZ.

QZ. What?

BRYAN. We don't need someone else here now, so just – send him home.

(Pause. **QZ** *stares at* **BRYAN.***)*

MATTHEW. Oh, I – I'm sorry, I didn't mean to –

QZ. *(to* **MATTHEW.***)* I left the backup disk in my trailer on the coffee table. Run up and get it for me?

(pause)

Matty, just give us a minute. Please.

(Pause. **MATTHEW** *nods, defeated.)*

MATTHEW. Uh – yeah. Okay.

*(***MATTHEW*** *gets up and exits.)*

QZ. Believe it or not, Bryan, while you've been off doing whatever the hell it is you've been doing, I've had a *life* here, and he's part of it. He's been here for years, he's put more work into this paper than you have.

(pause)

So just – don't mess with him, okay? He doesn't have anywhere else to go.

BRYAN. He doesn't have parents?

QZ. He has an alcoholic step-dad who threatened to kill him after catching him messing around with a boy from his class. You wanna send him home to that?

(The phone rings. Pause.)

When Jim died, he –.

(The phone rings again.)

He didn't have anyone left, so just –.

(The phone rings one last time, the answering machine picks up. **QZ** *turns to her computer.* **BRYAN** *awkwardly sits at a desk.)*

VOICE OF QZ. Hello love seekers! You've reached the message line for *The Few*'s personal ad section. Please leave your name, phone number, location, and your personal ad exactly as you would like it printed. Someone will call you back soon for payment information. Happy hunting!

(The answering machine beeps.)

MALE VOICE 2. Hello. I'm in Eastern Washington, 509-645-7842. Bradford. I am starting now. Seeking: one Christian lady for one man. I'm not crazy fanatic or using God here. I am a one-man-to-one-lady man. True blue. Looking for healthy relationship through God according to King James Version, not perverted or twisted. No cussers.

(The man hangs up. The answering machine beeps.)

(pause)

BRYAN. Do you want me to…?

(pause)

QZ. What?

BRYAN. You want that one in this week's issue?

QZ. What?

BRYAN. That ad. The one on the machine.

QZ. That's why we have a machine. Can you stop? I'm trying to do Tetris.

(A silence between them.)

BRYAN. So – what's his name?

*(**QZ** glances at him, keeps playing Tetris.)*

QZ. Really?

(pause)

Rick.

(pause)

BRYAN. How long? Have you guys been – ?

QZ. Couple years.

BRYAN. Sounds serious.

QZ. It is.

(**QZ** *pauses her game, turns to* **BRYAN**.)

He proposed to me.

(pause)

BRYAN. Really?

QZ. Yep.

(pause)

BRYAN. What'd you say?

(Silence. **QZ** *looks away.)*

QZ. Are you – seeing anybody?

BRYAN. Me? Oh, nah. Not since…

QZ. Nobody?

BRYAN. Nope.

QZ. Not *one?*

BRYAN. Not one.

QZ. Bullshit.

BRYAN. Seriously.

QZ. Why not?

(**BRYAN** *looks at* **QZ**.)

BRYAN. I don't know, it doesn't matter. It's all ephemeral anyway.

QZ. Uh-huh.

BRYAN. It doesn't last.

QZ. I know what ephemeral means, go to hell.

(**QZ** *goes back to her computer. Silence.* **BRYAN** *approaches her.*)

BRYAN. And I guess I just knew – I could never find someone as good as you.

(*Pause.* **QZ** *looks at him.*)

QZ. What the hell am I supposed to say to that?

BRYAN. I'm sorry –

QZ. You left me here *alone*, you realize that?

BRYAN. I know, I'm sorry –

QZ. Two days after *Jim's funeral*, you leave me here and –

(**MATTHEW** *re-enters.* **BRYAN** *and* **QZ** *stop.*)

MATTHEW. I, uh. I got the zip drive.

(*pause*)

Did you actually need the zip drive?

QZ. Yes, Matty, thank you.

(*Pause.* **MATTHEW** *puts the drive on* **QZ**'s *desk.* **BRYAN** *sits down at a desk, his head in his hands.* **QZ** *turns to her computer, presses play on the answering machine. It rewinds*).

(**MATTHEW** *cautiously approaches* **BRYAN**.)

MATTHEW. That's, um.

(*pause*)

It's just. That's sort of my desk. It's sort of my work station?

(**BRYAN** *and* **QZ** *don't move. The answering machine beeps.* **QZ** *types the ads as she listens.*)

(**MATTHEW** *awkwardly finds a folding chair, sets it up in a corner.*)

MALE VOICE 3. Wyoming, uh, Bruce, 307-239-5639. All-American in search of American honey. Like long walks and the second Harry Potter book, I-S-O L-T-R. All shapes and sizes welcome, please be under 60. Serious responses only.

(The answering machine beeps. Then suddenly:)

MATTHEW. *(louder than he intends)*
You guys this is so great!

(Pause. **BRYAN** *and* **QZ** *don't respond.)*

MALE VOICE 4. / Bobby, 406-785-6352. Montana, northwest. Fat and proud seeking –

MATTHEW. You know I was thinking – maybe we could invite some people over tonight, some of the truckers that used to come over here. I know some of them still live around here, they –

*(**QZ** hits stop on the answering machine, looks at* **MATTHEW**.)

I mean not like –. I mean it doesn't have to be about the *paper*, I just thought that people would like to see Bryan, that they'd like to –.

(pause)

It's just so great you're back.

QZ. What did you tell him?

BRYAN. What?

MATTHEW. I mean I was just thinking / that we could –

QZ. Wait, is *that* why you're back here? You think you can come back here and get me to change the paper?

BRYAN. *I'm not trying / to –*

MATTHEW. I just thought we could let people know that he's back –

QZ. The paper *finally* works, we're not messing with it. We're not inviting anyone over here, we're not doing *anything*.

BRYAN. Yeah, I mean God forbid – …

(Pause. **QZ** *looks at* **BRYAN**.*)*

QZ. I'm sorry, what was that?

BRYAN. Nothing.

QZ. No seriously, what?

(Pause. **BRYAN** *turns to* **QZ**.*)*

BRYAN. God forbid we try to do anything for these guys, right? God forbid we actually reach out to them like we used to, God forbid we actually put any energy into / making it –

QZ. Oh so I'm *lazy*, is that what I'm hearing? You left me with twelve grand of debt, which I have *almost* paid off, and you have the *balls* to say that I –

BRYAN. Oh congratulations, QZ, it's making money, very impressive. I seem to remember that when we started this paper, it wasn't about personal ads, it wasn't some stupid get-rich-quick scheme –

QZ. Oh yeah, because I'm so *rich* now.

MATTHEW. Oh crap guys, I didn't mean / to –

BRYAN. I don't even know why you still call it "The Few," might as well call it "Hot Trucker Monthly" or "Truckerbang" or – ...

(short pause)

Fuck it, forget it.

(Pause. **BRYAN** *turns away.)*

QZ. Fine. Let's do it. Let's invite the old gang over.

(pause)

MATTHEW. Wait really?

QZ. Why not? Haven't seen anyone for years, I bet they'd love to see you, right Bryan?

BRYAN. Look, you're right, the paper's fine the way it is, let's / not –

QZ. *(to* **BRYAN***)* Why don't you go into town and grab some Carlo Rossi, give everyone a call, we'll have a nice little community forum, just like we used to do with Jim. Right?

(pause)

Matty I've got this big headache so I'm gonna lie down for a while. Someone enter the rest of the messages.

*(**QZ** exits. Pause. **BRYAN** buries his head in his hands.)*

MATTHEW. Look, I know she's just being –. But I really think when she sees everyone, when she remembers –

BRYAN. You know I could really use a few minutes.

(pause)

Alone.

MATTHEW. Sure, I can – I can go do a few drop-offs, that's –. If you don't mind, we just need to get the messages entered into the –

BRYAN. Okay.

(pause)

MATTHEW. So you'll – … You'll make some calls?

(pause)

Bryan, really, when I run into these guys, when I talk to them… They need this. They need it back.

*(Pause. **BRYAN** nods at him.)*

*(**MATTHEW** smiles, then grabs a key ring and exits.)*

*(Silence. **BRYAN** stands up, looking around the office, takes a deep breath. He thinks.)*

*(Finally, he goes to **QZ**'s computer and presses play on the answering machine. He types the ads as he listens.)*

(The answering machine beeps.)

MALE VOICE 4. Bobby, 406-785-6352. Montana, northwest. Fat and proud seeking F. Easy going and friendly into all sorts of things. Ask any questions nothing offends me. I like sex it is important for me to have that. Thank you for reading.

(The answering machine beeps.)

FEMALE VOICE 2. It's, uh. Shit, I don't –.

(pause)

Nevermind, sorry.

(The answering machine beeps.)

MALE VOICE 5. Okay, Southern Idaho, Billy's the name, 208-345-0375. Here goes. Hey there! Hi there! Whoa there! Billy here looking for a female co-driver with at least two years experience. Intimate relationship not mandatory but welcome! Want to run 7000 plus miles. No druggies or drunks or fatties don't be offended that's just me. Whoa there!

(The answering machine beeps.)

FEMALE VOICE 2. Okay, uh. It's me, again. Sorry. Cindy, um. Idaho location, 208-347-3497. Cindy.

(pause)

I don't, um. I've never done one of these before, I. If this doesn't make sense, you can just delete it, I don't know what I'm doing.

(pause)

So, I'm a woman. Female. I'm forty-seven, and I used to drive an eighteen-wheeler but I had a little accident and I'm on disability now. Should I say things like that?

(pause)

I just – I think I just want someone who –. Can I start over?

(**BRYAN** *sighs, hits delete on the keyboard.*)

Okay, female. Forty-seven. I have been single for–
… Sorry, don't print that, shit. Female, forty-seven.
Looking for good person – good man. I have long
blonde hair and green eyes, and a few extra pounds
truth be told. Please be non-violent, and with a sense
of humor.

(pause)

I'm looking for –. Honesty.

(BRYAN *stops typing, listens.)*

I mean, I know that people lie, I know that. But I'm
looking for someone who is generally honest. When I
do stupid things I need someone to say "Cindy, don't
be stupid." But when I do things well, when I'm good
at something, I need someone to say, "Cindy, you did
that well. You're good at that thing." And I just don't
think that's asking too much. I think that I deserve that
much. I may not deserve a lot, but – …

(pause, a hint of desperation)

I guess I just feel like I woke up a couple days ago and
realized, for heck's sake it's gonna be a *new millennium*
in a few months, and what am I even doing? What have
I *ever* done? In my whole life, what have I ever – …?

(pause)

I'm sorry, just. I'm sorry, I'm wasting your time, I'm
sorry. I apologize. You can delete this, please just delete
this, I'm –.

*(She hangs up. The answering machine beeps, then is
silent.)*

(BRYAN *stares forward for a moment, then hits rewind
on the answering machine.)*

Scene Three

*(Later that night. **MATTHEW** has set up a few folding chairs. A large pile of old newspapers rests on one of the desks. **BRYAN** enters wearing a backpack and holding two large jugs of Carlo Rossi White Zinfandel.)*

MATTHEW. Hey.

(pause)

Party time! Heh.

*(**BRYAN** makes his way inside, puts the wine on a desk. He opens one, finds a glass, pours himself some wine. **BRYAN** pours a second glass, hands it to **MATTHEW**.)*

Oh, I. I don't really.

BRYAN. You allergic to this too?

MATTHEW. Well, yeah.

(pause)

BRYAN. What?

MATTHEW. Seriously. The tannins or something. My mom gave me a sip of red wine when I was a kid, my throat closed up.

BRYAN. What else are you allergic to?

MATTHEW. Cigarettes, red wine, some animals. That's it.

(pause)

Really, that's it.

*(**BRYAN** takes his backpack off, takes out a large bottle of bottom shelf whiskey. He opens the bottle, hands it to **MATTHEW**.)*

BRYAN. So you're not allergic to this then.

MATTHEW. *(taking the bottle)* Oh, um. Cool.

*(**BRYAN** motions for **MATTHEW** to drink from the bottle. **MATTHEW** takes a half-hearted swig of the whiskey.)*

BRYAN. Good?

MATTHEW. Yeah, it's –. Oak-y.

> (**BRYAN** *notices the old newspapers sitting in the corner.*)

Oh, that's. Those are like, mine. All the way back to the first issue. I thought it would be nice to look through some of them when people get here, or –

BRYAN. Yeah or we could just drink.

MATTHEW. Oh. Okay.

> (**BRYAN** *sits down, drinking his wine. He takes the whiskey bottle.*)

You know, um. I was reading that article that you wrote a few years ago about those motels in western Montana that you had stayed at when you were still trucking and it –

> (**BRYAN** *mixes some whiskey in with his wine.* **MATTHEW** *watches him.*)

Wow. Is that – should you be doing that?

BRYAN. QZ doesn't drink these anymore? She calls it a "Dirty Rossi." Used to be her favorite.

> (**BRYAN** *drinks.* **MATTHEW** *watches him for a moment. Then suddenly:*)

MATTHEW. *(quickly)* Anyway, the way you wrote about the trucker you had met at that one motel, the guy from the Philippines whose mother had just died the day before you talked to him? That was the one for me that was like – ... I didn't even know that writing could make me –. I'm being weird, *anyway* I was thinking that it could be a cool project or whatever to go back to some of those motels and do like a follow-up piece or whatever, and maybe it could also be a way that we could start getting to know more truckers, and –. Here, let me see if I can find it...

> (**MATTHEW** *goes to the stack of newspapers and starts rooting through them.*)

MATTHEW. *(cont.)* One of the motels you wrote about closed a couple years ago, but we could find some / other –

BRYAN. Okay look, I'm not –. Shit, I'm not trying to be rude. Please try to understand that I just don't care anymore. I really, really just *don't care.*

(silence)

MATTHEW. Why did you come back here?

BRYAN. You know I'd really appreciate the chance to just quietly get drunk if you don't / mind –

MATTHEW. No, seriously. If you don't care about this paper anymore, then why did you come back?

BRYAN. Frankly, kid, it's because I was tired and this is the only shelter I have legal right to anymore. I needed a place to stay, and if I have to pay my way by doing drop-offs and formatting personal ads, then fine.

MATTHEW. Bullshit.

(pause)

BRYAN. What was that?

MATTHEW. Bullshit. That's such bullshit, it's –

(pause)

Look you can act this way all you want, but – you started this thing for a / reason –

BRYAN. You know I gotta say, Matthew, you're starting to get a little irritating. And despite QZ's claim over this place, the fact is I still have the deed so I could have you out on your ass if it fucking pleases me. Okay?

*(Silence. **MATTHEW** stares at him, hurt. Finally he heads to the door, opening it.)*

Sorry. Fuck.

*(**MATTHEW** stops.)*

Sorry.

*(**MATTHEW** takes a few steps toward **BRYAN**, leaving the door open.)*

MATTHEW. Look, you gotta realize – when Jim fell asleep at the wheel, I didn't really have anyone?

BRYAN. I know –

MATTHEW. No, actually, you *don't* know, you –.

(*pause*)

When I lost Jim, this paper was the only part of him that I had left. When QZ let me move in, and I started working here, I thought you'd eventually come back, and when you did, I thought –. I don't know, I thought you'd – understand.

BRYAN. Guess I must be a pretty big disappointment.

MATTHEW. I mean I just don't –. Why did you leave? Was it because of what happened with Jim? Was it – ?

BRYAN. This isn't really something I'm eager to get into right now –

MATTHEW. Sorry but I've sort of been keeping your paper alive? For years? If you're ready to give up on it, can you just tell me *why*? Maybe you owe me that?

(*pause*)

Please.

BRYAN. Look, when we started this thing, it – …

(*pause*)

Jim and I started trucking around the same time. We both thought the money'd be good, thought it'd be nice to see the country. For a while it was, but – …

(*pause*)

It does something to you, driving that much. Jim and I were both doing runs across the whole country, easily saw forty-eight states between the two of us. After a while – you start to feel like you don't exist. Like you're never in a place long enough to even exist. You stop talking to people at gas stations and truck stops, you start avoiding the restaurants where the waitresses might recognize you, you start sleeping in the back of your cab just so you don't have to talk to a motel clerk. You go to diners and truck stops full of other long-haul guys, and you don't even look at each other.

(pause)

One night, Jim and I were both doing runs. I was in Utah, he was in North Carolina or something. He gives me a call, and he says he's at a truck stop – he says that he can't see anyone's faces. He says he's looking at people's faces, trying to see them – but he can't see anything.

(pause)

That night, I guess – QZ and I decided to do something.

MATTHEW. That's why you started the paper? For Jim?

BRYAN. Wasn't even a paper at first. I quit trucking, sunk the inheritance from my dad into this place. QZ quit her job at the gas station, and we both started spending all our time here. We just thought it could be a place where truckers could just – look at each other, talk. Remind each other that they still existed. QZ called it a "church without God." And it was.

(QZ appears in the open doorway. She smokes, being careful to blow the smoke outside. BRYAN and MATTHEW don't notice her.)

Pretty soon, long-haul guys were stopping by almost every night, just to talk. A lot of the time it was just daily stuff – long-distance marriages, gas prices, that kind of stuff. But every so often there'd be some guy, some trucker from some random corner of some random state who was *amazing*, come in and tell us a story about driving a tanker in the middle of a hurricane, or show us pictures he'd taken of sunrises at McDonald's in forty-three different states. And after a while, the three of us had the idea to just – write it down.

(pause)

Jim was still trucking, he'd drop off copies everywhere he could, every truck stop he came across. These little beacons scattered along the interstate, something to – … Something to remind us that we still existed.

(pause)

QZ. Hey.

*(***BRYAN*** and ***MATTHEW*** turn to **QZ**. She comes inside. Pause.)*

*(to **BRYAN**)*

You make me one?

*(***BRYAN*** pours a tumbler half full of wine, half full of whiskey. **QZ** takes one last puff and throws the cigarette outside. She goes to **BRYAN**, takes the cup.)*

Pretty speech, Bryan. Didn't think you had it in you anymore.

*(***QZ*** takes a drink.)*

BRYAN. Yeah, well.

QZ. *(re: the wine)* You got the White Zinfandel?

BRYAN. You always drank the White Zinfandel.

QZ. People change, Bryan. Tastes evolve. I'm a Cabernet Sauvignon girl now.

BRYAN. Well then.

MATTHEW. So I don't know when you told everyone to show up, but I thought we / could –

QZ. Yeah, Bryan, when's everyone getting here?

(pause)

BRYAN. I don't have anyone's number anymore.

QZ. Oh, really? So you're not feeling ashamed, that wouldn't have anything to do with it?

BRYAN. Can we please / just –

QZ. I don't blame you, I wouldn't wanna face them either. After abandoning everyone like that.

MATTHEW. Wait, so – wait no one else is coming?

(QZ sits down, drinking.)

BRYAN. *(to QZ)* You seen anyone lately?

QZ. Not for a while. People stopped coming over pretty quick after you left.

BRYAN. You ever hear from anyone? Cody or Jessica? Or / Ike – ?

QZ. Not for years. Everyone had to grow up, I guess.

(Pause. BRYAN looks at her.)

BRYAN. "Grow up"?

QZ. People had to realize this was just cheap group therapy and that they needed to get on with their lives –

BRYAN. C'mon, QZ.

QZ. I think a lot of them only came over here 'cause we'd give 'em free booze.

BRYAN. How can you say that? You loved this place, you had just as much faith in it as / we did –

QZ. And look what all that faith got us, huh?

(QZ drinks. BRYAN stares at her. Silence.)

What?

BRYAN. No, it's – nothing.

QZ. No, what?

BRYAN. You're just – different. From four years ago. You look different.

QZ. What the fuck is that supposed to mean?

MATTHEW. Okay so maybe the three of us could just talk? I mean QZ I know you don't want to change the whole paper and that makes / sense but –

QZ. How do I "look different"?

BRYAN. You just look – cynical, I guess. You never used to look so cynical.

(pause)

QZ. Well, having the supposed love of your life walk out on you two days after your best friend's funeral? That does tend to recalibrate your worldview a little bit.

MATTHEW. Okay! Maybe new topic?

QZ. Okay, sure. New topic: why the fuck is Bryan back after four years?

BRYAN. Okay QZ –

QZ. Oh right, he doesn't feel like talking about that right now, he doesn't want to tell us the reason he's back here, he just feels it's appropriate to come back, hold the deed to this place over my head, and then fucking tell me that I / "look cynical" –

BRYAN. I said / OKAY QZ.

QZ. – and try to ruin this paper after I've spent the last four years desperately trying to make it *profitable*, trying to make it into a *decent paper* –

BRYAN. Oh a "decent paper" is that what you've turned it into? Okay, let's see what you're working on for this month.

(BRYAN goes to QZ's computer.)

QZ. Get away from my computer, Bryan.

BRYAN. "Al Gore's Anti-Gun Presidential Platform." Nice QZ, real topical. / Well done.

QZ. I said get the fuck away from my / computer Bryan –

BRYAN. *(reading.)* "Gore wants us to believe that the second amendment did not exist, he – " *Jesus Christ*, what is it with you and mixing tenses?!

QZ. It's what people are talking about, Bryan, it sells papers – !

BRYAN. FINE. FORGET ABOUT IT, FORGET ABOUT WHAT WE MADE TOGETHER, FORGET IT EVER EXISTED.

*(**BRYAN** goes to the stack of papers. He opens one up, rips it up, and throws it on the floor.)*

MATTHEW. Wait – those are kind / of like, mine –

BRYAN. You believed in this paper / just as much as I did, you – ´

*(**BRYAN** grabs a clump of papers, crumpling them, throwing them to the floor.)*

MATTHEW. / *Please, stop, that's like my personal* –

QZ. You think there would even *be* a paper anymore if it wasn't for me?! We're actually *making money* now, we're almost ready to hire a web designer so we can start a / dating site –

BRYAN. If Jim could see what you've – …

*(**BRYAN** stops. **QZ** stares at him. Pause.)*

QZ. You wanna talk about Jim?

BRYAN. Don't –

QZ. No seriously, you wanna talk about Jim? Let's talk about Jim.

BRYAN. *Don't.*

QZ. How'd he turn out, Bryan?

*(Pause. **BRYAN** looks at her, pleading.)*

BRYAN. QZ, / *please* –

QZ. You can preach to this kid all night about our wonderful paper, about faith and all that horseshit, *but you know how it ended, you know what he* –.

(pause)

Tell him, Bryan.

(pause)

Tell him.

(Silence. They stare at one another.)

(finally:)

I'm going to bed.

(QZ exits. Silence.)

MATTHEW. I don't understand, what did – ?

(pause)

What did she mean, tell me what?

(Pause. BRYAN looks at MATTHEW.)

BRYAN. He left a note.

MATTHEW. What?

BRYAN. A suicide note. Jim left a suicide note, here. A few hours before he – …

(pause)

Four words. "can't live anymore sorry." No capital letters, no comma. He writes this note, then he gets in his truck, crosses the median on a bridge in North Dakota and takes out an entire family.

(pause)

"can't live anymore sorry."

(silence)

MATTHEW. No, I don't –. I don't believe you. They would have – the police would have found out, they would have –

BRYAN. Everyone just assumed he fell asleep, he had been driving all night, and he –. We – decided it was best to not tell anyone.

(MATTHEW wanders in disbelief for a moment. He looks at the papers on the ground, kicks them in frustration.)

(He looks at BRYAN for some response. BRYAN doesn't move. MATTHEW exits, slamming the door behind him.)

(A few moments pass. **BRYAN** *sits down, leans back in his chair, staring at the ceiling.)*

*(***MATTHEW*** *re-enters.)*

MATTHEW. I mean, look, you don't have to be like a prophet or something, you don't have to be fucking *Ghandi* to me. But you could –. You don't have to act like a complete dick and treat me like I'm some sort of – , like I'm not even worth your time. And I don't need you to be brilliant, I don't need you to –.

(pause)

Show it to me.

BRYAN. What?

MATTHEW. Show me the note. The note Jim left, show it to me.

BRYAN. Matthew, I don't / have –

MATTHEW. Then I don't believe you. I don't –.

(pause)

He did it on *purpose?*

(Silence. Then, in a fit of rage, **MATTHEW** *grabs a clump of papers and slams them down on a desk – they fly everywhere.)*

(The force of hitting the papers on the desk accidentally turns on the answering machine. **MATTHEW** *exits.)*

(The answering machine beeps.)

MALE VOICE 6. It's, uh –. Wait what am I supposed to –? Uh. Trent, I'm in –. Why do you need my phone number? Look don't print my name. Truckers call me Bent Nickel, just print that. No, uh, actually don't print that, just print –. Just print – hot trucker. Print hot trucker seeking –

(**BRYAN** *hits stop on the answering machine, then sits down. He stares up at the ceiling, the whiskey bottle in hand.*)

Scene Four

(The next morning.)

*(**BRYAN**, very drunk and unrested, sits in the same position as before, holding the now mostly empty bottle of whiskey. There is a large jug of antifreeze sitting on the desk in front of him. **BRYAN** is staring at it, motionless.)*

*(**MATTHEW** bursts into the office wearing his backpack. **BRYAN** keeps his eyes on the antifreeze.)*

*(**MATTHEW** stops, looks at **BRYAN**. He slams the door behind him as hard as he can. **BRYAN** doesn't move.)*

*(**MATTHEW** goes to his desk, petulantly throwing his backpack on top of it. He looks to **BRYAN**, who still doesn't react.)*

*(**MATTHEW** finally sits, turning on his computer. He looks around on his desk for a moment.)*

(silence)

MATTHEW. Where's the red floppy disk?

BRYAN. What?

MATTHEW. The red floppy disk. The one that's always right here, it has the master layout on it. It's important. Where is it?

BRYAN. I don't know.

(pause)

MATTHEW. Have you – … Did you sleep at all?

BRYAN. Not really.

MATTHEW. What are you doing with our antifreeze?

(no response)

There's a few stacks outside that need to be delivered still. The Denny's off 412, the Conoco off 401.

(re: the whiskey bottle)

But I guess I'll have to do them myself, just like every–!
Has QZ come in yet?

(*pause*)

BRYAN. You're working?

MATTHEW. Yes, I'm working, because I *have* to. This is how
I make money, this is how I *live*. Has QZ come in yet?

BRYAN. No.

(*pause*)

MATTHEW. I bought that disk with my own money, I
always leave it *right here*. Are you sure you didn't do
something with it?

BRYAN. I don't even know what you're / talking about –

MATTHEW. *A red floppy disk, it's square, and it's red, and / it –*

BRYAN. I heard you, I don't know / where –

MATTHEW. Forget it. Not like I have enough money to buy
another / one –

BRYAN. Is that what you're talking about?

(**BRYAN** *points to a red floppy disk sitting on the desk
next to* **MATTHEW.**)

MATTHEW. Oh.

(**MATTHEW** *takes the disk, puts it in his computer.*)

It's ten o'clock, where's QZ?

BRYAN. Gone.

MATTHEW. Where?

BRYAN. I don't know.

MATTHEW. Did she say if she was going to be back before
noon? I need her / to –

BRYAN. No but I doubt it.

MATTHEW. Why?

BRYAN. Because she took all her stuff.

(*pause*)

MATTHEW. What do you mean?

BRYAN. It was kind of amazing, around three in the morning she just starts packing up her station wagon. Managed to fit her whole bedroom in there, looked like. I watched her the whole time. She knew I was watching. She acted like she didn't know, but she knew.

(pause)

MATTHEW. Wait, what are you – what are you saying?

BRYAN. Allow me to simplify. QZ took her shit. She's gone. Probably for good.

*(**MATTHEW** pauses for a second, then bolts toward the door, exiting.)*

(A moment of silence.)

*(The phone rings. **BRYAN** doesn't move. The phone continues to ring, finally **BRYAN** stands up, wobbling. He goes to the phone, picks it up, then immediately hangs it up. The ringing stops, he sits back down.)*

*(**MATTHEW** re-enters.)*

MATTHEW. Oh my God. She's gone.

BRYAN. Yep.

MATTHEW. Where was she going?

BRYAN. I don't know.

MATTHEW. She didn't say anything to you?

*(**BRYAN** shakes his head, drinks the whiskey.)*

But we – I don't know what to do. I don't know how to… We're supposed to have our new issue ready to print by *tomorrow*, if we don't have it everyone's gonna want the money from their ad space back, and we don't even have enough money in the bank right now to pay the electric bill, I don't – …

(pause)

Shit. Oh shit.

(**BRYAN** *looks at* **MATTHEW**, **MATTHEW** *looks back. The phone begins to ring. Awkward pause.*)

What?

(**BRYAN** *takes a long drink of whiskey, then grabs the jug of antifreeze.*)

BRYAN. I guess Jim found a more dramatic way to do it, but this just seems a lot easier.

MATTHEW. Wait, what?

(**BRYAN** *looks at the antifreeze. The answering machine picks up,* **QZ**'s *greeting is heard.*)

VOICE OF QZ. / Hello love seekers! You've reached the message line for *The Few*'s personal ad section. Please leave your name, phone number, location, and your personal ad exactly as you would like it printed. Someone will call you back soon for payment information. Happy hunting!

BRYAN. Antifreeze uses either ethylene glycol or propylene glycol, propylene is poisonous but ethylene is *really fucking poisonous*, so –

MATTHEW. Wait –

BRYAN. *(examining the label.)*
And this – here – is ethylene. Perfect.

(*The greeting concludes, the answering machine beeps.*)

MALE VOICE 7. / Hi it's Kent F., you have all my info. Widowed S-W-M trucker in my early sixties.

BRYAN. I guess it'll probably still take a few hours, but.

MATTHEW. WHAT ARE YOU DOING?! I DON'T KNOW WHAT YOU'RE DOING!

BRYAN. I can do it outside –

(**BRYAN** *stumbles toward the door.*) ·

MATTHEW. *Please don't leave me here alone – !*

(BRYAN stops, halfway out the door, the antifreeze in one hand, the whiskey in the other. He looks at MATTHEW.)

MALE VOICE 7. Looking for any woman. Age and body type not important. Please – ... Please respond. I'm faithful. Please.

(The answering machine beeps.)

(MATTHEW and BRYAN remain motionless, looking at one another. Silence.)

MATTHEW. Could you – not drink that anti-freeze? Please?

(pause)

Look, she's gonna – QZ'll come back, she's probably just –

BRYAN. No she won't.

(pause)

I proposed to her.

MATTHEW. You – ?

BRYAN. The last letter I wrote to QZ, I proposed to her. She didn't answer, so – I came back. To get my answer. And now she's gone, so I suppose that must be a "no."

(pause)

MATTHEW. Wait, you – ? I thought Rick proposed to her –

BRYAN. If I responded to her ad, she never would have written me back, so – ... So I just – wrote her as Rick.

(Pause. BRYAN takes a long drink of the whiskey. He cradles the whiskey and the antifreeze in his arms.)

MATTHEW. Wait, you're – ? *You're Rick?*

BRYAN. It was more romantic in my head.

MATTHEW. You've been – ?

BRYAN. I told her I wasn't ready to meet her in person, just went through a personal tragedy or whatever, wasn't ready to see anyone… That part was true, I guess.

(BRYAN *downs the rest of the whiskey. The liquor has now gotten to him, he slowly starts to slide down to the ground.*)

MATTHEW. That's – … That's *awful* –

BRYAN. Yeah.

(BRYAN *is now on the ground, leaning up against the door. The whiskey bottle rolls out of his hand, he continues to clutch onto the antifreeze.*)

I am – *really* terrible at being a person.

(MATTHEW *goes to him.* BRYAN*'s eyes begin to close. Silence.*)

MATTHEW. Bryan?!

(BRYAN *is passed out, the antifreeze still in his arms.*)

(MATTHEW *looks down at him.*)

Scene Five

(That night. **BRYAN** *is in the same position as before –
everything is the same except for a large bike lock that
seals the front door shut. The antifreeze is no longer in
his arms and is nowhere in the space.)*

*(***BRYAN** *slowly starts to wake up. He is profoundly hung
over. He gets up, groaning, searching for water. He goes
to a water cooler, looks around for a cup, and when
he doesn't find it, he puts his mouth on the spout and
drinks for a while.)*

*(***MATTHEW** *enters from the back. He stares at* **BRYAN**
silently, stiff and intense.)

*(***BRYAN** *turns, sees* **MATTHEW**. **MATTHEW** *stares at
him.)*

BRYAN. What?

MATTHEW. I locked the door.

(pause)

BRYAN. What?

MATTHEW. I padlocked it with my bike lock.

BRYAN. Why?

MATTHEW. 'Cause you're not leaving. I'm not letting you
leave.

BRYAN. Alright, I'm really not feeling up for this, I'd really
just rather –

MATTHEW. Shut up.

(pause)

BRYAN. What?

MATTHEW. I said shut up. *Shut up.*

(pause)

BRYAN. I have no idea what's happening right now.

MATTHEW. What's happening is – you're gonna sit down and write. You're going to write an article, we're gonna format the personals, then we're gonna send it to the printers and do all the drop-offs. Okay?

BRYAN. No, we're not going to –.

(pause)

Look, I know this paper means something to you, but it's done, okay? Just – go home to your family or whatever, just –

*(**MATTHEW** pulls out a handgun, points it at **BRYAN**.)*

What?

MATTHEW. You're not leaving. There's enough food to last us a few days. You're going to *shut up*, and do what I say. We're not missing our deadline this month.

(pause)

BRYAN. Matthew, that's a BB gun. It's my old fucking BB gun.

MATTHEW. Yeah but if I shoot you it's *really* going to hurt.

*(**MATTHEW** pumps the BB gun five or six times.)*

*(**BRYAN** moves toward **MATTHEW**.)*

BRYAN. Okay, look. Just give me the key to the bike lock, I'll –

*(**MATTHEW** shoots **BRYAN** in the thigh. He cries out in pain.)*

JESUS CHRIST, that went into my fucking skin, you know that?!

MATTHEW. I KNOW! I'LL DO IT AGAIN.

*(**BRYAN** looks at his thigh.)*

BRYAN. I'm serious, it went into my skin!

MATTHEW. Fucking A!

*(**MATTHEW** pumps the BB gun again.)*

BRYAN. Alright give that to me *right now* –

(**MATTHEW** *shoots again, this time hitting* **BRYAN** *in the hand.*)

THAT HIT MY FUCKING FINGERNAIL!

MATTHEW. DON'T COME NEAR ME!

(**MATTHEW** *pumps the gun again,* **BRYAN** *lunges at him,* **MATTHEW** *easily evades him,* **BRYAN** *falls into a desk.*)

Dude you're not going to be able to catch me. I'm spry.

BRYAN. Look – I am *not* in the mood for this, do you understand? You are going to give me the key to that bike lock, you are going to go home, and –

MATTHEW. No, I'm not letting you kill yourself.

BRYAN. What?

MATTHEW. This morning you said you were going to kill yourself. I'm not letting you do that.

BRYAN. I was –. I was just *talking*, I don't know, I –

MATTHEW. You almost drank a jug of *antifreeze*. I'm not letting you kill yourself like Jim, I'm not letting the paper just *die*. I'm in charge now!

(**BRYAN** *looks around the room for a minute. He moves toward a printer, picking it up.*)

What are you doing?

BRYAN. I'm breaking a window and I'm getting out of here.

MATTHEW. Don't try it.

(**BRYAN** *moves toward a window with the printer.*)

I SAID DON'T TRY IT!

(**MATTHEW** *fires the gun at* **BRYAN**, *it hits him in the eye.* **BRYAN** *screams in pain, dropping the printer, grabbing his eye.*)

OH MY GOD OH MY GOD I'M SORRY I / DIDN'T MEAN TO!

BRYAN. YOU JUST FUCKING *BLINDED* ME –

MATTHEW. SORRY SORRY SORRY / SORRY – !

BRYAN. WHAT IS WRONG WITH YOU?! WHY DO YOU CARE SO MUCH ABOUT THIS FUCKING PAPER?!

MATTHEW. *BECAUSE IT'S ALL THAT I HAVE RIGHT NOW, DON'T YOU SEE THAT?!*

(*silence*)

(**BRYAN** *takes his hand off his eye, checking for blood. He finds a reflective surface, tries to examine his eye.*)

Did I really hit you right in the eye? Do you need to go to the hospital?

BRYAN. No, it's –. It's just scraped, it's –. Fucking BB is still in there, I can feel it when I move my eye. Jesus.

(**BRYAN** *sits down at a desk. Pause.*)

MATTHEW. Look, I'm sorry I shot your eye. But I can't –. I can't just like *go home*, my step-dad wouldn't even let me in the front door. And my mom's always on fucking pain pills, so she's not going to –. You can't just come back here and get drunk, chase QZ off, and shut down the paper because you don't care. *I care.*

(*pause*)

BRYAN. Look – I don't know what you expect me to write. I haven't been around for four years, it's not like I can offer anything to –

MATTHEW. I already know what you can write about.

BRYAN. Fantastic.

MATTHEW. The last four years. What you've been doing these past four years.

(**BRYAN** *looks away.*)

BRYAN. Look, we – our readers are totally different now, no one even knows who I am, no one –

MATTHEW. That doesn't matter. Just give them something honest, you tell them about the last four years. You can tell them about how you've been writing to QZ.

(pause)

BRYAN. I told you about that?

MATTHEW. Yeah.

BRYAN. Fantastic.

(**MATTHEW** *goes to him.*)

MATTHEW. Look, I just / think –

BRYAN. Could you put the goddam BB gun / down?!

MATTHEW. Sorry, sorry.

(**MATTHEW** *puts the BB gun on a desk.*)

Look, we can find new readers, build the paper up, once you tell them what you've learned, you know – what you've been doing all this time. Yeah?

(short pause)

BRYAN. I was working at a Perkins in Boise.

(silence)

MATTHEW. Like – the restaurant?

BRYAN. Yes. The restaurant. I wasn't traveling, I wasn't exploring, I wasn't searching out the fucking heart of America. I was a short order cook at Perkins. I lived in a motel across the parking lot that smelled *constantly* like burnt hair, and I drank myself to sleep every night. There's your article, stop the fuckin' presses.

(pause)

MATTHEW. You left – to work at a Perkins?

(pause) You're a *real asshole*, you know that?

BRYAN. Yes, I do know that, actually.

MATTHEW. No, I mean –. I thought you were doing something *important*, I thought you were like *searching* for something, or –

BRYAN. *(turning to* **MATTHEW***)* Okay, you wanna know what I've learned? Listen to me. When we started this paper we wanted to connect these guys, help them with their loneliness, blah blah blah, but the reality? The reality is, other people are *bullshit.*

(The phone begins to ring. **MATTHEW** *and* **BRYAN** *pay no attention to it. It continues to ring underneath the following.)*

Any sense of connection you have with another person is either a complete illusion or chemicals dancing around in your brain. I wasted years of my life trying to convince myself that we're not really alone, trying to convince Jim of that, and where did that get him?

(The answering machine picks up, **QZ***'s greeting is heard.)*

VOICE OF QZ. / Hello love seekers! You've reached the message line for *The Few*'s personal ad section. Please leave your name, phone number, location, and your personal ad exactly as you would like it printed. Someone will call you back soon for payment information. Happy hunting!

BRYAN. The sooner you accept the fact that you are completely alone, the sooner you accept that *everyone* is completely alone, the better off you'll be.

(The answering machine beeps.)

MATTHEW. You can't actually believe that.

QZ. *(on the machine) Hello?*

BRYAN. *Believe* that?

QZ. *(on the machine)* Matty, are you – ? Someone pick up?

(BRYAN *stops.* **MATTHEW** *and* **BRYAN** *stare at the machine.)*

(on the machine) Look, I'm –. I'm in the hospital, it's not a big deal, it's not –. I shouldn't have been driving last night after – ... Anyway I had

a little accident, I'm fine, but the car is –. I'm in Missoula, at – I don't remember what the name of the hospital is, it's –. Saint something, or –. Saint Patrick, it's Saint Patrick's, in Missoula. I need someone to come get me.

(*pause*)

Please pick up?

(*pause*)

Please. Pick up.

(**MATTHEW** *looks at* **BRYAN**. **BRYAN** *moves to the phone, picking it up.*)

BRYAN. Hi.

(*looking at* **MATTHEW**.)

You – …? Are you okay?

Scene Six

(The following morning. **QZ** *enters, followed by*
MATTHEW *who holds car keys.* **QZ** *has one arm in a*
sling and a few small bandages on her face.)

*(***MATTHEW** *hangs up the keys, closes the door. He goes to*
a computer, turns it on.)

MATTHEW. I mean look, they're gonna be pissed, we'll
probably lose some ad business, but as long as we get
the issue together by this afternoon then I think were
gonna be fine, I think we –

*(***MATTHEW** *looks at the computer. The screen is blank,*
the computer is unresponsive.)

Are you fucking kidding me?

*(***QZ** *stands in the middle of the trailer, looking around,*
as if for the first time. She looks up.)

*(***MATTHEW** *hits the computer a few times, trying to get*
it to start up.)

(to the computer)

Now, really? You're gonna do this *now?*

(pause)

Okay, that's – ... That's okay, it won't look good but I
can go to the Kinkos and copy some of the ads from
last month, it's not gonna look / right but –

QZ. That water stain is shaped exactly like Alaska.

(pause)

MATTHEW. What?

*(***QZ** *points up.)*

Oh. Okay?

QZ. You see that?

MATTHEW. Yeah?

QZ. When we started this place that water stain was nothing. Like a dot. It was Rhode Island, and now it's fucking Alaska.

(*Pause.* **MATTHEW** *goes to* **QZ**'s *computer.*)

MATTHEW. Look I don't know if you've finished your column for this month but if we can sort of throw it / together –

QZ. Matty.

MATTHEW. I can clean it up if you like, if it's not –. I can't find the file, is it – ...?

(**QZ** *goes to him.*)

If you don't have it finished then maybe we could run something from last year, or maybe we could / just –

QZ. You're fired.

(*pause*)

MATTHEW. What?

QZ. I know it doesn't feel like it, but believe me this is a gift.

(*pause*)

You can stay here as long as you like of course, I'm not kicking you out, but / you –

MATTHEW. Wait, you're – ? What are you doing?

(*pause*)

QZ. Matty. Don't you want to get out of here? Did you really think that this is where you were gonna spend the rest of your life?

(**MATTHEW** *stands up, paces a bit.* **QZ** *watches him. Pause.*)

I know that this paper meant something to you, but it's never going to turn back into what it used to be. I know that the only reason you worked here all this time is because you were hoping that eventually Bryan would come back and the paper / would –

MATTHEW. I worked here because I wanted to. I *wanted* to.

(pause)

You know, when you first let me move in here, and Bryan had already left, I figured –. I mean I thought you'd just shut the paper down, get a different job, but then – you didn't, you kept it going, and I was like – oh, she wants to stay. But then like another year went by, and I was like – oh. She *doesn't* want to stay here, she wants to *leave*. Why isn't she leaving?

QZ. You wanted me to leave you alone here, to run everything / by yourself?

MATTHEW. It wasn't for me. You know that, you didn't stay for me.

(pause)

I worked here because I *wanted* to, QZ, because I like it here, I feel *safe* here. But you – … I mean, you hate it here.

(pause)

You hate it here, right?

(a silence between the two of them)

(BRYAN *enters. He wears a makeshift eye-patch made from duct tape. He looks at* **QZ.***)*

(pause)

Okay, I'll –.

(pause)

I'll come back?

QZ. Thank you, Matty.

(MATTHEW *exits, shutting the door.* **QZ** *and* **BRYAN** *look at one another.)*

BRYAN. You get a DUI?

QZ. No, thank God. I was mostly sober by the time it happened, cop felt bad for me.

(pause)

BRYAN. I'm – glad you're okay. I wish you would have let me pick you up.

(Pause. QZ *looks at him.)*

QZ. Bryan, what are – ? What the fuck are we doing?

BRYAN. I don't know.

QZ. This place is trashed, we're not gonna make the next issue, my arm's in a sling, and what the fuck happened to your eye?

BRYAN. Matthew shot me.

QZ. Well good for him then.

(pause)

When we were in high school, I never thought we would turn out to be such awful people. How did we turn out to be such awful people?

(BRYAN *moves closer to her, still maintaining his distance.)*

BRYAN. QZ, I –. I really should tell you something.

(pause)

QZ. What?

(BRYAN *looks at* QZ. *Pause.)*

BRYAN. I don't know how to tell you this, I – ... Look, I should have told you this the second I came back here, but I was / worried –

QZ. *Why the hell did you have to propose to me?* We were doing *fine* – and then you fucking *propose?*

(pause)

BRYAN. Wait, you – ? Did you – ?

QZ. Jesus Christ, Bryan, of course I knew it was you.

(pause)

BRYAN. How long have you known?

QZ. Didn't take long to figure / out –

BRYAN. Shit, QZ, if you knew it was me then why didn't /
you – !

QZ. Well why did you pretend you were someone else in
the first place?!

BRYAN. Because I knew you'd actually respond to Rick!
You never would have written me back!

QZ. YOU'RE RIGHT, I WOULDN'T HAVE. YOU'RE AN
ASSHOLE. RICK'S A GOOD GUY.

BRYAN. But why didn't – ?! Why didn't you just *say*
something?!

QZ. WHY DIDN'T *YOU* SAY SOMETHING?

BRYAN. BECAUSE THOSE LETTERS WERE THE ONLY
GOOD THING LEFT IN MY LIFE.

(*silence*)

QZ. Yeah, well. Me too.

(*pause*)

Took me a few letters to realize it was you, actually.

BRYAN. What made you realize?

QZ. You used the word "beatific." You're such an asshole,
who uses that word?

(*pause*)

BRYAN. When I didn't hear back from you after my last
letter, I didn't know what to do –

QZ. That letter was beautiful, Bryan. I think it might be
the most beautiful thing you've ever written. Reading
it was – … It felt amazing, it felt *right.* Then I get to
the end, and you sign – "Rick." You propose to me,
and you sign – "Rick."

(*pause*)

QZ. *(cont.)* And when you first walked in here, and I saw you standing there I had this split second thought, like – *can we actually do this?* And I waited for you to say something, *anything*, but you just – …

(pause)

Did you really expect to just show up here and I'd fall into your arms? You *left* me.

BRYAN. I know, I'm sorry –

QZ. Why did you do that?

BRYAN. That doesn't matter / now –

QZ. No. No more of this shit, you're going to tell me.

*(Pause. **BRYAN** looks at her.)*

BRYAN. When Jim died and we found that note – …

(pause)

Everything we were doing here, this whole paper, even what I felt for you, it all felt so – … I wasn't some trucker poet, we hadn't made something real or meaningful here. We started this place because of Jim, we thought we were saving him all those years, saving all those other guys, but in the end it all just –

QZ. You think I didn't want to save him too? I *loved* him, I loved him since high school, just like you. We should have made him quit trucking the second you got that phone call from him, if I knew what he was capable of, I would have set fire to his rig myself –

BRYAN. He didn't do that because he was still trucking, QZ, it was bigger than that.

(pause)

When I left, I thought I'd just take the pick-up and drive around for a few days, maybe a week. Just to clear my head. After three or four days, I was on this rural highway out in Wyoming in the middle of the night, and I hadn't seen any other cars for miles and miles, and these two little headlights show up in the distance. And we get closer, and closer, and suddenly it was like – all I had to do was one simple movement. From there…

(**BRYAN** *holds his hand out, miming a steering wheel at twelve o'clock.*)

To there.

(**BRYAN** *moves his hand to ten o'clock.*)

And that would be it. And the car gets right next to me, and I swear to God it took *everything in me* not to do it.

(*silence*)

QZ. You know about a week before Jim died, Kelly and Dave and those guys were over here, you remember that?

BRYAN. I think so?

QZ. Jim had just done that run up to Alaska, he was telling us about tipping over on that mountain pass with all those pigs in his truck? He felt so bad for them being out in the cold, he packed two dozen of them into his cab with him so they wouldn't freeze to death?

(**BRYAN** *smiles.*)

BRYAN. Yeah.

QZ. He was so – *happy*, being here with all of us, he was actually – … Later that night, he told me that when he was out trucking, he would think about this place as much as he could, because whenever he thought about us, he knew for certain that there were other people in the world.

(*pause*)

We saved him as much as we could, Bryan. I don't know what happened to him out there, but when he was with us, when he was *here* – he wasn't a murderer. He was our best friend.

(pause)

BRYAN. So where does that leave us?

(silence)

*(Pause. **QZ** gets up, goes to the filing cabinet and takes out the large stack of letters from before. She puts them down in front of **BRYAN**, sits next to him.)*

*(**BRYAN** looks at them for a moment, not saying anything. He exits momentarily, returns with a similar stack of letters. He brings them back to **QZ** and sets them next to hers.)*

(silence)

QZ. My *God*, we are so much better on paper, aren't we?

BRYAN. Yeah. We are.

*(**QZ** and **BRYAN** laugh a bit. **BRYAN** reaches a hand across the desk toward **QZ**. They hold hands for a moment, looking at one another.)*

So...?

(pause)

QZ. What?

BRYAN. You never answered my question.

(silence)

QZ. Well, so. Ask me.

(pause)

BRYAN. I already did.

QZ. That was Rick. I want Bryan to propose to me.

(pause)

BRYAN. QZ.

(pause)

Will you marry / me?

QZ. No.

(Pause. They slowly release one another. **QZ** *looks at him.)*

No.

*(***QZ***. takes a few breaths, then goes to the door, taking a keyring.)*

I'm gonna take the pick-up, they've got my car at a lot over in Missoula. All my stuff's still in it. Hopefully it's not all ruined.

(pause)

BRYAN. You coming back?

(pause)

QZ. I've lived in the same thirty-mile area my entire life, and when I was driving yesterday, when I just left? It felt amazing, like some big change was coming, something soon. New millennium, whatever.

(pause)

Then – I ended up in a ditch, in the hospital, and then – back here. Where I always am. Back here, with you. New millennium, same old shit, I guess.

(Pause. **QZ** *looks at the keys in her hand.)*

BRYAN. Who knows? Maybe something will happen. Maybe we get to start over.

(pause)

QZ. I'm not coming back, Bryan.

(Silence. **QZ** *goes to her stack of letters, taking it in her arms.)*

I'm gonna tell Matty he can take the Honda, and he – … Just make sure he's gonna be okay, yeah?

(pause)

BRYAN. Yeah.

(She heads toward the door, then turns back to **BRYAN**.*)*

QZ. I'll write you.

   *(***QZ*** *exits.)*

Scene Seven

(Several days later. **MATTHEW** *stands in the trailer with a couple packed duffel bags.)*

*(***BRYAN*** *enters from the back, wearing a proper eyepatch.)*

MATTHEW. *(re: the eyepatch)* Ahoy there!

(awkward pause)

Is it – okay?

BRYAN. It's fine. Doctor said I'll be able to get rid of the patch it in a couple days.

MATTHEW. It's kinda cool looking.

BRYAN. Yeah, I know.

(pause)

MATTHEW. I'm really sorry for shooting you in the eye?

BRYAN. It's fine.

MATTHEW. No but seriously.

BRYAN. I deserved it. It's fine.

(pause)

Do you know where you're going to go?

MATTHEW. Haven't completely decided. I have a cousin in Eugene, she's a veterinarian. She said I can stay with her.

BRYAN. Sounds nice.

MATTHEW. Yeah, I don't –. I was thinking about maybe just doing some wandering, you know? Maybe just drive around, take some odd jobs. Maybe travel a bit before / I –

BRYAN. You really, really should go to Eugene.

(pause)

MATTHEW. Yeah, I guess –. I guess that's smart.

(pause)

MATTHEW. *(cont.)* Are you sure about me taking the Honda? I mean the only other car is the Subaru, and I don't think that runs very well, I wouldn't take it too far.

BRYAN. It's fine.

MATTHEW. You gonna be able to do the drop-offs in that thing?

BRYAN. Well, I doubt we have much of a paper anymore. Gonna have to refund all the advertisers. Issue was due days ago and we don't have anything.

MATTHEW. Yeah we do.

BRYAN. What?

*(**MATTHEW** takes an edition of the paper out of his duffel.)*

What is this?

MATTHEW. It's nothing special, sorta sloppy. But I managed to pull it together. I just got rid of the content, made it all personals.

(points at the paper.)

See it's a "special singles edition." I'd actually be surprised if it didn't sell better than our normal editions.

*(**BRYAN** looks through the paper.)*

BRYAN. When the hell did you do this?

MATTHEW. I just threw it together, brought it to the printers that day. They did it pretty quick, they owed me.

(pause)

There's still some drop-offs that need to be done. They're in the Subaru, should be pretty self-explanatory.

BRYAN. *(re: the paper)* My God there are a lot of personal ads here.

MATTHEW. Yeah, busy month. A lot more on the machine, too.

(*pause*)

You sure you're gonna be okay out here all alone?

BRYAN. I'll be fine.

(*short pause*)

MATTHEW. You – gonna keep the paper going?

(*pause*)

BRYAN. Suppose I gotta survive somehow.

MATTHEW. You think you'll write anything?

(*pause*)

BRYAN. I think we've got enough to fill a paper every month. Don't need to confuse it with anything I'd write.

(*pause*)

MATTHEW. Look, I know it didn't work, I know that –. But this paper – it really did help me. You know that, right?

BRYAN. I know, it's / okay –

MATTHEW. Please, just – I've been trying to do this ever since you came back here, just –.

(**MATTHEW** *takes out his wallet, takes out a folded-up newspaper clipping. He looks at it.*)

(*reading*)

"You can find us in between Wallace and Mullan, off exit 419, about two miles south of the gas station. If you ask us what our agenda is, we'll tell you that we don't know. If you ask us why we started a newspaper for truckers, we'll tell you it's because we had to. Because after over fifteen years of driving the length of the country over and over, alone, spending / years – "

BRYAN. Matthew, / c'mon –

MATTHEW. Just –. Please.

(continues reading.)

"...spending years sleeping in parking lots that all blend together, eating at McDonald's and Wendy's that all look and smell the same, passing truck after truck on the interstate knowing each driver felt just as isolated as you, you start to feel like you don't exist. So we had to do something. Something for the few of us who need it. Something to remind us, the few of us who live this way, that we still exist."

(stops reading, pause)

I know you made this paper for truckers, but –. Growing up here, being – who I am... I sort of felt like I didn't exist either. But reading what you wrote every month – helped. A lot.

(pause)

So just – thank you.

(MATTHEW *puts the clipping on the desk in front of* **BRYAN***. He grabs his duffel.)*

BRYAN. Listen, uh.

(BRYAN *grabs a pencil, searches for a piece of paper to write on. He grabs a newspaper from the ground, tears off a piece, starts writing.)*

I went to high school with this girl – Allison Spector. You know the poetry club I started at Mullan High?

MATTHEW. Yeah.

BRYAN. Well, it was with her. More her idea than mine. Anyway, last I heard she was still in the – field, or whatever. She had a press out in Portland, just a small little thing.

MATTHEW. Are you serious?

BRYAN. Last time I did a run through Portland we met up, she was still publishing. I don't remember what it was called, but just look her up and tell her – I sent you. Like I said, I have no idea if she still does it anymore, that was years ago, but –.

(He hands the piece of paper to **MATTHEW**.*)*

(pause)

Why don't you read me something?

MATTHEW. What do you mean?

BRYAN. Read me one of your poems or whatever.

(pause)

C'mon, you made me listen to my own stuff, just read me something.

MATTHEW. No, I – I can't.

BRYAN. Yeah, you can, c'mon.

MATTHEW. But it's not – I've never even read this stuff out loud.

BRYAN. That's okay, just try it.

MATTHEW. No, I don't even know what I'd read to you, I / don't –

BRYAN. *Jesus* would you stop being such a little pussy and just *read me something?*

MATTHEW. OKAY okay. Geez.

*(**MATTHEW** reaches into his duffel, taking out a notebook. He flips a few pages, he lands on one.)*

Okay, I can –. I guess I can read this one.

(pause)

It's a Tanka.

(pause)

BRYAN. What?

MATTHEW. It's like – it's this form of poetry, I think it's Japanese? It's five lines, the first and third lines have five syllables, and the rest / have –

BRYAN. Okay stop it, you're ruining it, stop. Just read it.

MATTHEW. Sorry.

(reading.)

"Stray cat on my porch
gray striped eyes stare, then vanish;
triggered memories
a thought I don't recognize
a smell I had forgotten."

(pause)

That's it.

(pause, defeated.)

It's a Tanka.

(Silence. MATTHEW looks away.)

BRYAN. It's really good.

MATTHEW. Really?

BRYAN. Yeah. It's really, really good.

(Pause. MATTHEW smiles, puts it back in his bag.)

MATTHEW. It's just a stupid poem, whatever.

(pause)

Look, not to be annoying but – you're not going to kill yourself, right? I mean you're like – done with that idea, right?

(pause)

BRYAN. Yeah, pretty much.

MATTHEW. That's really good!

BRYAN. Yeah.

MATTHEW. You must feel so optimistic!

(pause)

BRYAN. I just – need to accept that my life isn't as noble or important or exciting as I thought it would be once. I just need to grow up.

(pause)

MATTHEW. I mean that's – sort of optimistic, I guess. 'Cause now there's nowhere to go but up.

*(**MATTHEW** grabs his duffel, heads toward the door. He gives **BRYAN** a wave as he exits, **BRYAN** waves back.)*

*(**BRYAN** sits for a minute, silent.)*

(He stands up, surveys the room, then looks down at all the papers on the ground. He begins to collect them, grabs a trash bag, and shoves them into the bag.)

(After he bags a few handfuls he moves to the answering machine and pushes play.)

*(The answering machine rewinds, then beeps and begins to play messages as **BRYAN** collects the papers.)*

MALE VOICE 8. Tom, 541-235-2950, I'm in Eastern Oregon. Nice trucker, does seven thousand plus, CDL Class A with hazmat. Looking for nice woman for L-T-R, good hygiene, good looking in face. I enjoy the finer things in life, looking for a woman who does also.

*(The answering machine beeps. **BRYAN** realizes the bag is too small to collect all the papers, he exits outside momentarily, returns with a large outdoor trash barrel.)*

(The answering machine beeps.)

MALE VOICE 9. Uh. Uhhhhhh –.

*(The answering machine beeps. **BRYAN** continues to clean up the papers, throwing them into the trash barrel.)*

FEMALE VOICE 3. Mandy, Idaho location, 208-348-9467. I would like to learn how to drive a truck but I do not have money to go to driving school. I have no family to help me. I'm single and 40 and want to learn how to drive. No dogs, no cats. Very sincere. Please help.

(The answering machine beeps. As he's cleaning, **BRYAN** *finds the original edition of* The Few *that* **MATTHEW** *had in Scene Three. He regards it for a moment, then throws it into the barrel.)*

FEMALE VOICE 4. Montana, 406-343-2043, my name's Jessie. Full-figured woman with big breasts looking for man. Just got out of an L-T-R, looking to start a new one. I don't know how to swim. Send me a message and we will meet and see what happens. Please only men interested in large breasted women.

(The answering machine beeps.)

*(***BRYAN** *has now collected all of the papers, he places the trash bag on the floor and continues to clean up various items – the broken printer, the empty whiskey bottle, etc.)*

(The answering machine beeps.)

FEMALE VOICE 5. Um, it's –. Ugh, fuck, forget it.

(The answering machine beeps. **BRYAN***. finds the BB gun from before, looks at it.)*

FEMALE VOICE 6. Enjoy warm oil massages question mark. I can help exclamation point. Eastern Washington near I-90. 509-239-6792. Come to me I will rub you from head to toe and make you feel amazing. I will ease your tension and satisfy your needs.

(The answering machine beeps. **BRYAN** *moves to a desk, opens various drawers looking for a place to put the gun. He opens a drawer, stops when he sees what's in it. He reaches inside and pulls out the jug of antifreeze.)*

(He sits down at the desk, holding the antifreeze.)

MALE VOICE 10. Uh, northern Utah, 'bout two hours outside Logan, 435-393-2274. Fifties, attractive looking for same. I like trucks, motorcycles, dogs, country music. I do car shows, Sturgis, flea markets.

(**BRYAN** *puts the antifreeze onto the desk in front of him.
He looks at it for a moment, then leans forward, burying
his head in his hands.*)

Twice divorced, looking for a stable relationship. I
smoke, no drugs, no alcohol. No kids. Looking forward
to your reply.

(*The answering machine beeps.*)

FEMALE VOICE 2. Hi, it's, uh. It's Cindy? I called before. It's
Cindy. I left a real long personal, and then I asked you
not to print it, but you did anyway, and –.

(*pause*)

So I'm actually not calling with a personal ad, this is
more of a –.

(*pause*)

When I saw you printed my ad, at first I was so mortified,
I had no idea what people would think, or – … I was
ready to call you back and give you a piece of my mind,
I'll tell you what. But – yesterday, I got a response from
this person, this man.

(*pause*)

We talked for almost five hours on the phone last
night, past midnight, which for *me* is just –. I mean I
don't really honestly remember the last time I talked
to someone for that long. And he's really just – good.
He's good. He's gentle, and he listens, and he – …

(**BRYAN** *lifts his head up, listening.*)

So I – I'm calling to say thank you. I mean look, I don't
know if this is gonna – *amount* to anything, or –. I've
learned not to count on anything in my life. But even
if we never talk again, even if it's just that one phone
call last night, it really did – help. I felt like I was in a
pretty bad way when I left that ad, and I didn't really
know how it was all gonna end, but –. You really did
something for me, I told you not to print the ad, but
you did anyway, and you didn't even charge me…

(**BRYAN** *looks at the clipping* **MATTHEW** *left on the desk, takes it in his hand, looking at it. Pause.*)

Right now – at this moment? The future is looking better for me. Much better. It's like I can see the sun again. And I hope that everyone over in your office or whatever, I hope you're all – good. Thank you. Really, just – thank you.

(*The answering machine beeps, and is silent.*)

(**BRYAN** *looks up, taking in a deep breath. He exhales.*)

End of Play